I0649121

George Colman, Samuel Foote

The Nabob

A Comedy, in Three Acts

George Colman, Samuel Foote

The Nabob
A Comedy, in Three Acts

ISBN/EAN: 9783744767927

Printed in Europe, USA, Canada, Australia, Japan

Cover: Foto ©Andreas Hilbeck / pixelio.de

More available books at **www.hansebooks.com**

THE

N A B O B;

A COMEDY.

WRITTEN by Mr. FOOTE,

PUBLISHED by Mr. COLMAN.

[Price One Shilling and Sixpence.]

THE

NABOB;

A COMEDY,

IN THREE ACTS.

AS IT IS PERFORMED AT THE

THEATRE-ROYAL in the HAYMARKET.

WRITTEN BY THE LATE

SAMUEL FOOTE, *Efq.*

AND NOW PUBLISHED BY

Mr. COLMAN.

LONDON,
Printed by T. Sherlock,
For T. CADELL, in the Strand.

MDCCLXXVIII.

PROLOGUE,

Spoken by Mr. FOOTE,

At the Theatre-Royal in DUBLIN,

On the 19th of November, 1773.

UPWARDS of twenty years are fled and wafted
    Since in this fpot your favour firft I tafted.
Urg'd by your fmiles thro' various realms to roam,
The Mufe now brings her motley cargo home;
For frugal Nature, with an equal hand,
Beftows peculiar gifts to every land.
To France fhe gave her rapid repartee,
Bows, and *bons mots*, fibs, fafhions, flattery,
Shrugs, grins, grimace, and fportive gaiety:
Arm'd with the whole artillery of love,
Latium's foft fons poffefs the powers to move:
Humour, the foremoft of the feftive crew,
Source of the comic fcene, fhe gave to you;
Humour, with arched brow, and leering eye,
Shrewd, folemn, fneering, fubtle, flow and fly;
Serious herfelf, yet laughter ftill provoking,
By teafing, tickling, jeering, gibing, joking:
Impartial gift, that owns nor rank nor birth!
'Tis theirs who rule the realm, or till the earth;
Theirs who in fenates wage the wordy war,
And theirs whofe humble lot conducts the car:
If aught deriv'd from her adorns my ftrain,
You gave, at leaft difcover'd firft, the vein.
Should wide experience, or maturing age,
Have brought or mirth or moral to the ftage,

To

To you, the patrons of the wilder fong,
The chaſter notes in juſtice muſt belong:
But ſhould infirmities with time conſpire,
My force to weaken or abate my fire,
Leſs entertainment may ariſe to you,
But to myſelf leſs danger will enſue.
If age contracts my muſcles, ſhrills my tone,
No man will claim thoſe foibles as his own;
Nor, if I halt or hobble thro' the ſcene,
Malice point out what citizen I mean:
No foe I fear more than a legal fury,
Unleſs I gain this circle for my jury.

DRAMATIS

DRAMATIS PERSONÆ.

Sir MATTHEW MITE,	Mr. Foote.
Sir JOHN OLDHAM,	Mr. Gentleman.
Mr. THOMAS OLDHAM,	Mr. Aickin.
YOUNG OLDHAM,	Mr. Du-Bellamy.
Mr. MAYOR,	Mr. Parsons.
TOUCHIT,	Mr. Baddeley.
FIRST ANTIQUARIAN,	Mr. Loyd.
SECOND ANTIQUARIAN,	Mr. Hamilton.
SECRETARY,	Mr. Davis.
RAPINE,	Mr. Lings.
NATHAN,	Mr. Castle.
MOSES,	Mr. Jacobs.
JANUS, } PUTTY, }	Mr. Weston.
CONSERVE,	Mr. Fearon.
WAITER,	Mr. Ward.

LADY OLDHAM,	Mrs. Egerton.
SOPHY,	Miss Ambrose.
Mrs. MATCH'EM;	Mrs. Gardner.
CROCUS,	Miss Craven.

Beadle, Servants, &c.

THE

THE

NABOB.

ACT I.

A Chamber.

Enter Lady Oldham and Sir John Oldham.

Lady Oldham.

NOT a fyllable more will I hear!
Sir John. Nay, but, my dear——
L. Old. I am amazed, Sir John,
at your meannefs! or that you could
fubmit to give his paltry propofals fo much as a
reading!

Sir John. Nay, my dear, what would you have,
had me done?

L. Old. Done? returned them with the contempt they deferved. But, come, unfold! I am
calm: Reveal the pretty project your precious
head has produced.

B   *Sir*

Sir John. Nay, my dear, as to that, my head produced——

L. Old. Nay, I don't wonder that fhame has tied up your tongue! But, come; I will fpare the confufion, and tell you what you would fay. Here, Lady Oldham, Sir Matthew Mite has juft fent me a letter, modeftly defiring that, in return for the ruin he has brought on me and my houfe, I would be fo kind as to beftow upon him my darling daughter, the hopes of my——And is it poffible you can be mean enough to think of fuch an alliance? Will you, Sir John, oblige me with an anfwer to a few fhort queftions?

Sir John. Without doubt.

L. Old. I fuppofe you confider yourfelf as fprung from a family at leaft as ancient as any in the county you live in?

Sir John. That I fancy will not be denied.

L. Old. Nor was it, I fancy, difhonoured by an alliance with mine?

Sir John. My Lady, the very reverfe.

L. Old. You fucceeded, Sir, to a patrimony, which though the liberal and hofpitable fpirit of your predeceffors would not fuffer to encreafe, yet their prudence took care fhould never be diminifhed?

Sir John. True.

L. Old. From the public and private virtues of
your

your anceſtors, the inhabitants of the neighbour-
ing borough thought their beſt and deareſt in-
tereſts in no hands ſo ſecure as in theirs ?

Sir John. Right.

L. Old. Nor till lately were they ſo tainted by
the faſhion of the times, as to adopt the egregious
abſurdity, That to be faithfully ſerved and pro-
tected above, it was neceſſary to be largely
bribed and corrupted below ?

Sir John. Why, I can't ſay, except now and
then a bit of veniſon, or an annual dinner, they
have ever put me to any great——

L. Old. Indulge me yet a moment, Sir John !
In this happy ſituation, did the laſt year chear-
fully cloſe ; our condition, though not opulent,
affluent, and you happy in the quiet poſſeſſion
of your family honours.

Sir John. There is no gainſaying of that.

L. Old. Now, look at the diſmal, ſhocking
reverſe !

Sir John. There is but too much reaſon in what
your ladyſhip ſays.

L. Old. And conſider, at the ſame time, to
whom you are obliged.

Sir John. Why, what could we do ? your
ladyſhip knows there was nobody more againſt
my giving up than yourſelf.

L. Old. Let me proceed. At this criſis,

preceded

preceded by all the pomp of Afia, Sir Matthew Mite, from the Indies, came thundering amongft us ; and, profufely fcattering the fpoils of ruined provinces, corrupted the virtue and alienated the affections of all the old friends to the family.

Sir John. That is nothing but truth.

L. Old. Compelled by the fame means to defend thofe that were employed in attacking your intereft, you have been obliged deeply to encumber your fortune; his fuperior addrefs has procured a return; and probably your petition will complete the ruin his oppofition began.

Sir John. Let us hope all for the beft.

L. Old. And who can tell, but you may be foon forced to part with your patrimony, to the very infolent worthlefs individual, who has been the author of your diftrefs ?

Sir John. I would fooner perifh, my Lady !

L. Old. Parallel inftances may be produced; nor is it at all unlikely, but Sir Matthew, taking a liking to your family manfion, has purfued this very method to compel you to fell it,

Sir John. It is, my dear, to avoid this neceffity that I wifh you to give his letter a reading.

L. Old. Is it poffible, not to mention the meannefs, that you can be weak enough to expect any real fervice from that infamous quarter ?

Sir

Sir John. Who can tell, my love, but a confcioufnefs of the mifchief he has done us, may have roufed fome feelings that——

L. Old. His feelings! will he liften to a private complaint, who has been deaf to the cries of a people? or drop a tear for particular diftrefs, who owes his rife to the ruin of thoufands?

Sir John. Well, Lady Oldham, I find all that I fay fignifies nothing.—But here comes brother Thomas; two heads are better than one; let us take his opinion, my love.

L. Old. What need of any opinion? the cafe is too clear; nor indeed, if there had been a neceffity for confulting another, fhould I have thought your brother the propereft man to advife with on the occafion.

Sir John. And why not? there is not a merchant whofe judgment would be fooner taken.

L. Old. Perhaps not, on the value of merchandize, or the goodnefs of a Bill of Exchange: But there is a nicety, a delicacy, an elevation of fentiment, in this cafe, which people who have narrowed their notions with commerce, and confidered during the courfe of their lives their intereft alone, will fcarce comprehend.

Enter Mr. Thomas Oldham.

Thomas. So, fifter! what! upon your old topic, I find?

L. Old.

L. Old. Sir!

Thomas. Some pretty comparifons, I fuppofe, not much to the honour of trade.

L. Old. Nay, brother, you know I have always allowed merchants to be a ufeful body of men; and confidered commerce, in this country, as a pretty refource enough for the younger fhoots of a family.

Thomas. Exceedingly condefcending, indeed! And yet, fifter, I could produce you fome inftances where the younger fhoots have flourifhed and throve, when the reverend trunk has decayed.

L. Old. Perhaps, brother Thomas ——

Thomas. Nay, nay, don't let us revive our antient difputes!—You feem warm; no mifunderftanding, I hope?

Sir John. No, no; none, in the leaft: You know, my lady's temper's apt to be lively now and then.

Thomas. Nay, fifter—But, come! what has occafioned this mighty debate?

Sir John. You know, brother, how affairs ftand between Sir Matthew and us,

Thomas. Well!

Sir John. He has fent us here a kind of a compromife; I don't know well what to call it; a fort of a treaty.

Thomas.

Thomas. That in your hand?

Sir John. Yes; and I can't prevail on my lady to give it a reading.

Thomas. And why not?

L. Old. To what end?

Thomas. A very natural one; in order to know the contents.

L. Old. Of what importance can they be to us?

Thomas. That the letter will tell you. But furely, Lady Oldham, you are rather too nice. Give it me!

Sir John. Is it your ladyfhip's pleafure?

Thomas. Pfha! here's a rout, indeed!—One would be apt to fufpect that the packet was peftilential, and came from the Archipelago, inftead of the Indies. Now let us fee what this formidable memorial contains! [*opens the letter.*
'" To Sir John Oldham. Sir Matthew Mite hav
" ing lately feen, at Lady Levant's rout, the
" eldeft Mifs Oldham, and being ftruck with
" her perfonal charms, propofes to her father
" the following treaty."

L. Old. A very monarchical addrefs!

Thomas. " *Imprimis;* Upon a matrimonial
" union between the young lady and him, all
" hoftilities and contention fhall ceafe, and Sir
" John be fuffered to take his feat in fecurity."

L. Old.

L. Old. That he will do, without an obligation to him.

Thomas. Are you, fister, certain of that?

L. Old. You don't harbour the least doubt of our merits?

Thomas. But do they always prevail?

L. Old. There is now, brother Thomas, ho danger to dread; the reftraint the popular part of government has in this inftance laid on itfelf; at the fame time that it does honour to them, diftributes equal juftice to all.

Thomas. And are you aware what the expence will be to obtain it?—But, pray, let me proceed!—" Secondly, as Sir Matthew is bent upon
" a large territorial acquifition in England, and
" Sir John Oldham's finances are at prefent a lit-
" tle out of repair, Sir Matthew Mite will make
" up the money already advanced in another
" name, by way of future mortgage upon his
" eftate, for the entire purchafe, five lacks of
" roupees."

L. Old. Now, Sir John! was I right in my guefs?

Sir John. Your ladyfhip is never out.—But, brother Thomas, thefe fame lacks—to what may they amount?

Thomas. Sixty thoufand, at leaft.

Sir John. No inconfiderable offer, my lady.

L. Old.

L. Old. Contemptible! But pray, Sir, proceed.

Thomas. " Or if it should be more agreeable
" to the parties, Sir Matthew will settle upon
". Sir John and his Lady, for their joint lives,
" a jagghire."

Sir John. A jagghire?

Thomas. The term is Indian, and means an annual income.

L. Old. What strange jargon he deals in!

Thomas. His stile is a little Oriental, I must own; but most exceedingly clear.

L. Old. Yes, to Coffim Ali-Khan, or Mier Jaffeir. I hope you are near the conclusion.

Thomas. But two articles more. [*reads*] " And
" that the principals may have no cares for the
" younger parts of their family, Sir Matthew
" will, at his own expence, transport the two
" young ladies, Miss Oldham's two sisters, to
" Madrass or Calcutta, and there procure them
" suitable husbands."

L. Old. Madrass, or Calcutta!

Thomas. Your patience, dear sister!—" And
" as for the three boys, they shall be either made
" supercargoes, ships' husbands, or go out cadets
" and writers in the Company's service."

L. Old. Why, he treats my children like a parcel of convicts: Is this their method of supplying their settlements?

Thomas.

Thomas. This, with now and then a little kidnapping, dear fifter.—Well, madam, you have now the means of getting rid of all your offspring at once : Did not I tell you, the paper was worth your perufal ? You will reply to his wifh ; you can have no doubts, I fuppofe.

L. Old. Not the leaft, as I will fhew you. [*Tears the letter.*] And, if Sir John has the leaft fpirit or pride, he will treat the infolent principal as I do his propofals.

Thomas. But that method, as things ftand, may not be altogether fo fafe. I am forry you were fo hafty in deftroying the letter : If I remember rightly, there is mention made of advancing money in another man's name.

L. Old. We have been compelled to borrow, I own ; but I had no conception that he was the lender.

Thomas. That's done by a common contrivance ; not a country lawyer but knows the doctrine of transfer.—How much was the fum ?

Sir John. Ten thoufand pounds.

Thomas. And what, Sir John, were the terms ?

Sir John. As I could give no real fecurity, my eftate being fettled till my fon John comes of age, I found myfelf obliged to comply with all that was afked.

Thomas. A judgment, no doubt.

Sir

Sir John. They divided the sum, and I gave them a couple.

Thomas. Which will affect not only your perfon, but perfonal property; fo they are both in his power.

Sir John. Too true, I am afraid!

Thomas. And you may be fent to a gaol, and your family turned into the ftreets, whenever he pleafes.

L. Old. How! Heaven forbid!

Thomas. Not the leaft doubt can be made.—This is an artful project: No wonder that fo much contrivance and cunning has been an over-match for a plain Englifh gentleman, or an inno-cent Indian. And what is now to be done? Does your daughter Sophy know of this letter?

L. Old. Sir John?

Sir John. It reached my hands not ten minutes ago.

Thomas. I had fome reafon to think, that, had you complied, you would not have found her very eager to fecond your wifhes.

L. Old. I don't know that, brother: Young girls are eafily caught with titles and fplendor; magnificence has a kind of magick for them.

Thomas. I have a better opinion of Sophy. You know, Lady Oldham, I have often-hinted, that my boy was fond of his coufin; and poffibly

my

my niece not totally averfe to his wifh; but you have always ftopp'd me fhort, under a notion that the children were too nearly allied.

L. Old. Why, brother, don't you think——

Thomas. But that, fifter, was not the right reafon; you could have eafily digefted the *coufins*, but the *compting-boufe* ftuck in his way: Your favourite maxim has been, that citizens·are a diftinct race, a fort of creatures that fhould mix with each other.

L. Old. Blefs me, brother, you can't conceive that I——

Thomas. Nay, no apology, good Lady Oldham! perhaps you have a higher alliance in view; and let us now confider what is to be done. You are totally averfe to this treaty?

L. Old. Can that be a queftion?

Thomas. Some little management is neceffary, as to the mode of rejection: As matters now ftand, it would not be prudent to exafperate Sir Matthew.

L. Old. Let Sir John difcharge the debt due to him at once.

Thomas. But where fhall we get materials?

L. Old. Can that be a difficult tafk?

Thomas. Exceedingly fo, as I apprehend: But few can be found to advance fo large a fum on fuch flender fecurity; nor is it to be expected, indeed,

indeed, unlefs from a friend to relieve, or a foe
to ruin.

L. Old. Is it poffible Sir Matthew can have
acted from fo infernal a motive, to have advanced
the money with a view of diftreffing us deeper?

Thomas. Sir Matthew is a profound politi-
cian, and will not ftick at trifles to carry his
point.

L. Old. With the wealth of the Eaft, we have
too imported the worft of its vices. What a
horrid crew!

Thomas. Hold, fifter! don't gratify your re-
fentment at the expence of your juftice; a general conclufion from a fingle inftance is but in-
different logick.

L. Old. Why, is not this Sir Matthew———

Thomas. Perhaps as bad a fubject as your
paffion can paint him: But there are men from
the Indies, and many too, with whom I have
the honour to live, who difpenfe nobly and with
hofpitality here, what they have acquired with
honour and credit elfewhere; and, at the fame
time they have increafed the dominions and
wealth, have added virtues too to their country.

L. Old. Perhaps fo: But what is to be done?
Suppofe I was to wait on Sir Matthew myfelf.

Thomas. If your ladyfhip is fecure of commanding your temper.

Sir

Sir John. Mercy on us, brother Thomas, there's no such thing as trusting to that!

L. Old. You are always very obliging, Sir John! if the embassy was to be executed by you——

Thomas. Come, come, to end the dispute, I will undertake the commission myself.

L. Old. You will take care, brother, to make no concessions that will derogate from——

Thomas. Your dignity, in my hands, will have nothing to fear.—But should not I see my niece first? she ought to be consulted, I think.

Sir John. By all means.

Thomas. For, if she approves of the knight, I don't see any thing in the alliance so much to be dreaded.

L. Old. I will send Sophy to her uncle directly; but I desire the girl may be left to herself; no undue influence! [*Exit.*

Thomas. The caution was needless.

Sir John. Why, really, now, brother, but that my lady's too warm, I don't see any thing so very unreasonable in this same paper here that lies scattered about. But, I forget, did he mention any thing of any fortune he was to have with the girl?

Thomas. Pho! a paltry consideration, below his concern.

Sir

Sir John. My lady herfelf muft own there is fomething generous in that.

Thomas. Will you ftay and reprefent the cafe to Sophy yourfelf?

Sir John. She is here!

Enter Sophy.

Your uncle, child, has fomething to fay to you: You know he loves you, my dear, and will advife you for the beft. [*Exit.*

Thomas. Come hither, Sophy, my love! don't be alarmed. I fuppofe my lady has opened to you, that Sir Matthew has fent a ftrange kind of a romantic letter.

Sophy. But fhe did not feem, Sir, to fuppofe that it deferved much attention.

Thomas. As matters now ftand, perhaps more than fhe thinks. But come, my good girl, be explicit: Suppofe the affairs of your family fhould demand a compliance with this whimfical letter, fhould you have any reluctance to the union propofed?

Sophy. Me, Sir? I never faw the gentleman but once in my life.

Thomas. And I don't think that would intereft you much in his favour.

Sophy. Sir!

Thomas.

Thomas. No prepoffeffion ? no prior object that has attracted your notice ?

Sophy. I hope, Sir, my behaviour has not occafioned this queftion.

Thomas. Oh, no, my dear ; it naturally took its rife from the fubject. Has your coufin lately been here ?

Sophy. Sir !

Thomas. Tom Oldham, my fon ?

Sophy. We generally fee him, Sir, every day.

Thomas. I am glad to hear that: I was afraid fome improper attachment had drawn him from the city fo often of late.

Sophy. Improper ! I dare fay, Sir, you will have nothing of that kind to fear from my coufin.

Thomas. I hope not : And yet I have had my fufpicions, I own ; but not unlikely you can re-move 'em : Children rarely make confidants of their fathers.

Sophy. Sir !

Thomas. Similarity of fentiments, nearnefs of blood, and the fame feafon of life, perhaps may have induced him to unbofom to you.

Sophy. Do you fuppofe, Sir, that he would difcover to me, what he chofe to conceal from fo affectionate a father ?

Thomas. Nay, prithee, Sophy, don't be grave ! What, do you imagine I fhould think his pre-

ferring

ferring your ear to mine, for a melting paſſionate tale, any violent breach of his duty?

Sophy. You are merry, Sir.

Thomas. And who knows but you might re-pay the communication with a ſimilar ſtory? You bluſh, Sophy.

Sophy. You are really pleaſed to be ſo very particular, that I ſcarce know what anſwer to make.

Thomas. Come, my good niece, I will perplex you no longer: My ſon has concealed nothing from me; and did the completion of your wiſhes depend on my approbation alone, you would have but little to fear: But my lady's notions are ſo very peculiar, you know, and all her prin-ciples ſo determined and fixed——

Sophy. The merits of my couſin, which ſhe herſelf is not ſlow to acknowledge, and time, might, I ſhould hope, ſoften my mother.

Thomas. Why then, my dear niece, leave it to time, in moſt caſes the ableſt phyſician. But let your partiality for Tom be a ſecret!—I muſt now endeavour to learn when I can obtain an audience from Sir Matthew.

Sophy. An audience from *him*?

Thomas. Yes, child; theſe new gentlemen, who from the caprice of Fortune, and a ſtrange

D   chain

chain of events, have acquired immoderate wealth, and rose to uncontroled power abroad, find it difficult to descend from their dignity, and admit of any equal at home. Adieu, my dear niece! But keep up your spirits! I think I foresee an event that will produce some change in our favour.   [*Exeunt.*

Sir Matthew Mite's Hall.

Janus and Conserve discovered.

Conf. I own the place of a porter, if one can bear the confinement—And then, Sir Matthew has the character of—[*low tap.*] Use no ceremony, Mr. Janus; mind your door, I beseech you.

Janus. No hurry! keep your seat, Mr. Conserve; it's only the tap of a tradesman: I make those people stay till they collect in a body, and so let in eight or ten at a time; it saves trouble.

Conf. And how do they brook it?

Janus. Oh, wonderfully well, here with us. In my last place, indeed, I thought myself bound to be civil; for as all the poor devils could get was good words, it would have been hard to have been sparing of them.

Conf. Very considerate!

Janus.

Janus. But here we are rich; and as the fellows don't wait for their money, it is but fair they fhould wait for admittance.

Conf. Or they would be apt to forget their condition.

Janus. True.

Conf. Upon the whole, then, you do not regret leaving my lord?

Janus. No; Lord Levee's place had its fweets, I confefs; perquifites pretty enough: But what could I do? they wanted to give me a rider.

Conf. A rider?

Janus. Yes; to quarter Monfieur Friffart, my Lady's valet de chambre, upon me; fo you know I could not but in honour refign.

Conf. No; there was no bearing to be rid by a Frenchman; there was no ftaying in after that.

Janus. It would have been quoted as a precedent againft the whole corps.

Conf. Yes. Pox on 'em! our mafters are damned fond of encroachments. Is your prefent duty fevere?

Janus. I drudge pretty much at the door; but that, you know, is mere bodily labour: But then, my mind is at eafe; not obliged to rack my brain for invention.

Conf. No?

Janus,

Janus. No; not near the lying here, as in my laſt place.

Conf. I ſuppoſe not, as your maſter is but newly in town; but you muſt expeᴄt that branch to encreaſe.

Janus. When it does, I ſhall inſiſt the door be done by a deputy.   [*Two raps.*

Conf. Hark! to your poſt!

Janus. No; ſit ſtill! that is ſome aukward body out of the city; one of our people from Leadenhall-Street; perhaps a direᴄtor; I ſha'n't ſtir for him.

Conf. Not for a direᴄtor? I thought he was the commanding officer, the Great Captain's captain.

Janus. No, no; quite the reverſe; the tables are turned, Mr. Conſerve: In acknowledgment for appointing us their ſervants abroad, we are ſo obliging as to make them direᴄtors at home.

[*A loud rapping.*

Conf. That rap will rouſe you, I think.

Janus. Let me take a peep at the wicket. Oh, ph! is it you, with a pox to you? How the deuce came your long legs to find the way hither?—I ſhall be in no haſte to open for you.

Conf. Who is it?

Janus. That eternal teizer, Sir Timothy Tall-boy.

boy. When once he gets footing, there is no
such thing as keeping him out. .

Conf. What, you know him then?

Janus. Yes, rot him, I know him too well!
he had like to have loft me the beft place I ever
had in my life.

Conf. How fo?

Janus. Lord Lofty had given orders on no
account to admit him. The firft time, he got by
me under a pretence of ftroking Keeper the
houfe-dog ; the next, he nick'd me by defiring
only juft leave to fcratch the poll of the parrot,
Poll, Poll, Poll! I thought the devil was in him
if he deceived me a third; but he did, notwithftanding.

Conf. Prithee, Janus, how?

Janus. By begging to fet his watch by Tompion's
clock in the Hall; I fmoaked his defign, and laid
hold of him here: [*taking hold of his coat.*] As
fure as you are alive, he made but one leap from
the ftairs to the ftudy, and left the fkirt of his
coat in my hand?

Conf. You got rid of him then?

Janus. He made one attempt more; and, for
fear he fhould flip by me, (for you know he is
as thin as a flice of beef at Marybone-Gardens),
I flapped the door in his face, and told him, the
dog was mad, the parrot dead, and the clock
stood;

ftood; and, thank Heaven, I have never fat eyes on him fince. [*Knock louder.*

Conf. But the door !

Janus. Time enough.—You had no particular commands, mafter Conferve ?

Conf. Only to let you know that Betfy Robins has a rout and fupper on Sunday next.

Janus. Conftant ftill, Mr. Conferve, I fee. I am afraid I can't come to cards; but fhall be fure to attend the repaft. A nick-nack, I fuppofe ?

Conf. Yes, yes; we all contribute, as ufual: The fubftantials from Alderman Sirloin's; Lord Frippery's cook finds fricafees and ragouts; Sir Robert Bumper's butler is to fend in the wine, and I fhall fupply the defert.

Janus. There are a brace of birds and a hare, that I cribbed this morning out of a bafket of game.

Conf. They will be welcome.—[*Knock louder.*] But the folks grow impatient !

Janus. They muft ftay till I come.—At the old place, I fuppofe ?

Conf. No; I had like to have forgot ! Betfy grew fick of St. Paul's, fo I have taken her a houfe amongft the new buildings; both the air and the company is better.

Janus. Right,

Conf.

Conf. To say truth, the situation was difagreeable on many accounts. Do you know, though I took care few people fhould behave better at Chriftmas, that becaufe he thought her a citizen, the houfekeeper of Drury-Lane Theatre, when his mafter mounted, refufed her a fide-box?

Janus. No wonder Mifs Betfy was bent upon moving.—What is the name of her ftreet?

Conf. Rebel-Row: It was built by a meffenger who made his market in the year forty-five. But fhall Mifs Robins fend you a card?

Janus. No, no; I fhall eafily find out the place. [*Knock.*] Now let us fee; who have we here? Gads my life, Mrs. Match'em! my mafter's amorous agent: It is as much as my place is worth to let her wait for a minute.

[*Opens the door. Exit Conf.*

Enter Mrs. Match'em, fome Tradefpeople, who bow low to Janus, and Thomas Oldham.

Match. So, Sir! this is pretty treatment, for a woman like me to dangle at your gate, furrounded by a parcel of tradefpeople!

Janus. I beg pardon; but, madam——

Match. Suppofe any of my ladies had chanced to drive by: In a pretty fituation they'd have feen me! I promife you I fhall make my complaints to Sir Matthew.

Janus. I was receiving fome particular commands from my mafter.

Match. I fhall know that from him. Where is he? let him know I muft fee him directly; my hands are fo full I have not a moment to fpare.

Janus. At that door the groom of the chamber will take you in charge; I am fure you'll be admitted as foon as announced.

Match. There is as much difficulty to get a fight of this fignior, as of a member when the parliament's diffolved !   [*Exit.*

Janus. Soh! what, you have brought in your bills? damned punctual, no doubt! The fteward's room is below.—And, do you hear? when you are paid, be fure to fneak away without feeing me.

All Tradef. We hope you have a better opinion——

Janus. Well, well, march! [*Exe. Tradefmen.*] So, friend; what is your bufinefs, pray?

Thomas. I have a meffage to deliver to Sir Matthew.

Janus. You have? and pray what is the purport?

Thomas. That's for his ear alone.

Janus. You will find yourfelf miftaken in that.

Thomas. How?

Janus.

Janus. It muſt make its way to his, by paſſing thro' mine.

Thomas. Is that the rule of the houſe?

Janus. Ay; and the beſt way to avoid idle and impertinent pratlers.

Thomas. And of that you are to judge?

Janus. Or I ſhould not be fit for my poſt. But, you are very importunate; who are you? I ſuppoſe a Jew broker, come to bring my maſter the price of the ſtocks?

Thomas. No.

Janus. Or ſome country couſin, perhaps?

Thomas. Nor that neither.

Janus. Or a voter from our borough below? we never admit them but againſt an election.

Thomas. Still wide of the mark.—[*Aſide.*] There is but one way of managing here; I muſt give the Cerberus a ſop, I perceive.—Sir, I have really buſineſs with Sir Matthew, of the utmoſt importance; and if you can obtain me an interview, I ſhall think myſelf extremely obliged.
[*Gives money.*

Janus. As I ſee, Sir, by your manner, that it is a matter of moment, we will try what can be done; but you muſt wait for his levee; there is no ſeeing him yet.

Thomas. No?

Janus. He is too buſy at preſent; the waiter

at Almack's has juſt brought him home his macaroni dreſs for the hazard-table, and is inſtructing him to throw the dice with a grace.

Thomas. Then where can I wait?

Janus. If you will ſtep into that room, I will take care to call you in time. [*Exit Mr. Old.*] —*Looking at the money.*] A good ſenſible fellow! At firſt ſight, how eaſily one may be miſtaken in men! [*Exit.*

ACT

ACT II.

A Chamber. Sir Matthew Mite in his gaming dress, a Waiter attending.

Mite.

MAIN and chance?

Waiter. Five to nine, please your honour.

Mite. I am at all that is set. How must I proceed?

Waiter. With a tap, as the chances are equal; then raise the box genteelly and gently, with the finger and thumb.

Mite. Thus?

Waiter. Exactly, your honour. Cinque and quater: You're out.

Mite. What is next to be done?

Waiter. Flirt the bones with an air of indifference, and pay the money that's set.

Mite. Will that do?

Waiter. With a little more experience, your honour.

Mite. Then pass the box to my neighbour?

Waiter. Yes; or you make a back hand, if you please.

E 2 *Mite.*

Mite. Cou'dn't you give me some general rules ? for then, you know, I might practise in private.

Waiter. By all means. Seven, Sir, is better nicked by a stamp.

Mite. So ?

Waiter. Yes. When you want to throw six and four, or two cinques, you must take the long gallery, and whirl the dice to the end of the table.

Mite. Thus ?

Waiter. Pretty well, please your honour. When your chance is low, as tray, ace, or two deuces, the best method is to dribble out the bones from the box.

Mite. Will that do ?

Waiter. Your honour comes rapidly on.

Mite. So that, perhaps, in a couple of months, I shall be able to tap, flirt, stamp, dribble, and whirl, with any man in the club ?

Waiter. As your honour has a genius, you will make a wonderful progress, no doubt : But these nice matters are not got in a moment; there must be parts, as well as practice, your honour.

Mite. What ! parts for the performance of this ?

Waiter. This ? Why, there's Sir Christopher Clumsey, in the whole losing his fortune, (and

I believe

I believe he was near a twelvemonth about it) never once threw, paid, or received, with one atom of grace.

Mite. He muſt have been a dull devil, indeed.

Waiter. A mere dunce! got no credit by loſing his money; was ruined without the leaſt reputation.

Mite. Perhaps ſo. Well, but, Dick, as to the oaths and phraſes that are moſt in uſe at the club?

Waiter. I have brought them here in this paper: As ſoon as your honour has got them by heart, I will teach you when and in what manner to uſe them.

Mite. [*after looking at the paper.*] How long do you apprehend before I may be fit to appear at the table?

Waiter. In a month or ſix weeks. I would adviſe your honour to begin in the Newmarket week, when the few people left do little better than piddle.

Mite. Right: So I ſhall gain confidence againſt the club's coming to town.

Enter Servant.

Serv. Mrs. Crocus, from Brompton, your honour.

Mite. Has ſhe brought me a bouquet?

Serv.

Serv. Your honour?

Mite. Any nofegays, you blockhead?

Serv. She has a boy with a bafket.

Mite. Shew her in! [*Exit Servant.*]—Well, Dick, you will go down to my fteward, and teach him the beft method of making a rouleau. And, do you hear? let him give you one for your pains.

Waiter. Your honour's obedient! You'd have me attend every morning?

Mite. Without doubt: It would be madnefs to lofe a minute, you know.   [*Exit Waiter.*

Enter Mrs. Crocus.

Well, Mrs. Crocus; let us fee what you have brought me.   Your laft bouquet was as big as a broom, with a tulip ftrutting up like a ma-giftrate's mace; and, befides, made me look like a devil.

Crocus. I hope your honour could find no fault with the flowers? It is true, the polyan-thufes were a little pinched by the eafterly winds; but for pip, colour, and eye, I defy the whole parifh of Fulham to match 'em.

Mite. Perhaps not; but it is not the flowers, but the mixture, I blame. Why, here now, Mrs. Crocus, one fhould think you were out of your fenfes, to cram in this clump of jonquils!

Crocus.

Crocus. I thought your honour was fond of
their fmell.

Mite. Damn their fmell! it is their colour I
talk of. You know my complexion has been
tinged by the Eaft, and you bring me here a
blaze of yellow, that gives me the jaundice.
Look! do you fee here, what a fine figure I cut?
You might as well have tied me to a bundle of
fun-flowers!

Crocus. I beg pardon, your honour!

Mite. Pardon! there is no forgiving faults of
this kind. Juft fo you ferved Harry Hectic;
you ftuck into his bofom a parcel of hyacinths,
though the poor fellow's face is as pale as a
primrofe.

Crocus. I did not know——

Mite. And there, at the opera, the poor crea-
ture fat in his fide-box, looking like one of the
figures in the glafs-cafes in Weftminfter-Abbey;
dead and dreft!

Crocus. If gentlemen would but give directions, I would make it my ftudy to fuit 'em.

Mite. But that your curfed climate won't let
you. Have you any pinks or carnations in
bloom?

Crocus. They are not in feafon, your honour.
Lillies of the valley——

Mite. I hate the whole tribe! What, you
want

want to dress me up like a corpse! When shall you have any rose-buds?

Crocus. The latter end of the month, please your honour.

Mite. At that time you may call.

Crocus. Your honour has no further commands?

Mite. None. You may send nosegays for my chairmen, as usual. [*Exit Mrs. Crocus.*] Piccard! Here, take that garland away: I believe the woman thought she was dressing a may-pole. Make me a bouquet with the artificial flowers I brought from Milan.

Enter Servant.

Serv. Would your honour please to see Madam Match'em?

Mite. Introduce her this instant.

Enter Mrs. Match'em.

My dear Match'em! Well, what news from Cheapside?

Match. Bad enough; very near a total defeat.

Mite. How so? you were furnished with ample materials.

Match. But not of the right kind, please your honour. I have had but little intercourse with that part of the world: My business has chiefly

lain

lain on this fide of the Bar; and I was weak
enough to think both cities alike.

Mite. And arn't they?

Match. No two nations can differ fo widely!
Though money is fuppofed the idol of merchants, their wives don't agree in the worfhip.

Mite. In that article I thought the whole
world was united.

Match. No; they don't know what to do
with their money; a Pantheon fubfcription, or
a mafquerade ticket, is more negotiable there
than a note from the Bank.

Mite. What think you of a bracelet, or a
well-fancied aigret?

Match. I fhould think they muft make their
way.

Mite. I have fent fome rough diamonds to
be polifhed in Holland; when they are returned,
I will equip you, Match'em, with fome of thefe
toys.

Match. Toys? how light he makes of thefe
things!—Blefs your noble and generous foul!
I believe for a trifle more I could have obtained
Lady Lurcher laft night.

Mite. Indeed?

Match. She has been preffed a good deal to
difcharge an old fcore, long due to a knight
from the North; and play-debts, your honour

knows, there is no paying in part : She feemed deeply diftreffed; and I really believe another hundred would have made up the fum.

Mite. And how came you not to advance it?

Match. I did not chufe to exceed my commiffion ; your honour knows the bill was only for five.

Mite. Oh, you fhould have immediately made it up; you know I never ftint myfelf in thefe matters.

Match. Why, had I been in cafh, I believe I fhould have ventured, your honour. If your honour approves, I have thought of a project that will fave us both a good deal of trouble.

Mite. Communicate, good Mrs. Match'em !

Match. That I may not pefter you with applications for every trifle I want, fuppofe you were to depofit a round fum in my hands.

Mite. What, Match'em, make you my banker for beauty ? Ha, ha, ha !

Match. Exactly, your honour. Ha, ha, ha !

Mite. Faith, Match'em, a very good conceit.

Match. You may depend on my punctuality in paying your drafts.

Mite. I don't harbour the leaft doubt of your honour.

Match. Would you have me proceed in Patty Parrington's bufinefs ? She is expected from Bath in a week.

Mite. And what becomes of her aunt?

Match. That Argus is to be left in the country.

Mite. You had better fufpend your operations for a while. Do you know, Mrs. Match'em, that I am a-going to be married?

Match. Married? your honour's pleafed to be pleafant: That day I hope never to fee.

Mite. The treaty wants nothing but her friends' ratification; and I think there is no danger of their with-holding that.

Match. Nay, then, the matter is as good as concluded: I was always in dread of this fatal ftroke!

Mite. But, Match'em, why fhould you be fo averfe to the meafure?

Match. Can it be thought, that with dry eyes I could bear the lofs of fuch a friend as your honour? I don't know how it is, but I am fure I never took fuch a fancy to any man in my life.

Mite. Nay, Match'em!

Match. Something fo magnificent and princely in all you fay or do, that a body has, as I may fay, a pleafure in taking pains in your fervice.

Mite. Well, but prithee, child——

Match. And then, when one has brought matters to bear, no after-reproaches, no grum-blings from parties, fuch general fatisfaction on all fides! I am fure, fince the death of my huf-

band,

band, as honeſt a man, except the thing he died
for——

Mite. How came that about, Mrs. Match'em ?

Match. Why, Kit was rather apt to be careleſs,
and put a neighbour's name to a note without
ſtopping to aſk his conſent.

Mite. Was that all ?

Match. Nothing elſe. Since that day, I ſaw
no mortal has caught my eye but your honour.

Mite. Really, Match'em ?

Match. I can't ſay, neither, it was the charms
of your perſon—though they are ſuch as any
lady might like—but it was the beauties of your
mind, that made an impreſſion upon me.

Mite. Nay, prithee, Match'em, dry up your
tears ! you diſtreſs me ! Be perſuaded you have
nothing to fear.

Match. How !

Mite. Why, you don't ſuppoſe that I am
prompted to this projeƈt by paſſion ?

Match. No ?

Mite. Pho ! no ; only wanted a wife to complete my eſtabliſhment ; juſt to adorn the head
of my table.

Match. To ſtick up in your room, like any
other fine piece of furniture ?

Mite. Nothing elſe ; as an antique buſt or a
piƈture.

Match.

Match. That alters the cafe.

Mite. Perhaps, I fhall be confined a little at firft ; for when you take or bury a wife, decency requires that you fhould keep your houfe for a week : After that time, you will find me, dear Match'em, all that you can wifh.

Match. Ah ! that is more than your honour can tell. I have known fome of my gentlemen, before marriage, make as firm and good refolutions not to have the leaft love or regard for their wives ; but they have been feduced after all, and turned out the pooreft tame family fools !

Mite. Indeed ?

Match. Good for nothing at all.

Mite. That fhall not be my cafe.

Enter Servant.

Serv. Your honour's levee is crouded.

Mite. I come. Piccard, give me my coat !—I have had fome thoughts of founding in this town a feraglio; they are of fingular ufe in the Indies : Do you think I could bring it to bear ?

Match. Why, a cuftomer of mine did formerly make an attempt; but he purfued too violent meafures at firft ; wanted to confine the ladies againft their confent ; and that too in a country of freedom.

Mite. Oh, fy ! How the beft inftitutions may fail, for want of a man proper to manage !

Match.

354582

Match. But your honour has had great experience. If you would beſtow the direction on me——

Mite. Impoſſible, Match'em! in the Eaſt we never confide that office to your ſex or complexion. I had ſome thoughts of importing three blacks from Bengal, who have been properly prepared for the ſervice; but I ſha'n't venture till the point is determined whether thoſe creatures are to be conſidered as mere chattels, or men.   [*Exeunt.*

A Saloon.

Enter Mayor, Touchit, Nathan, Moſes, &c.

Serv. Walk in, gentlemen! his honour will be preſently here.

Touchit. Do you ſee, Mr. Mayor? look about you! here are noble apartments!

Mayer. Very fine, very curious, indeed! But, after all, Maſter Touchit, I am not ſo over-fond of theſe Nabobs; for my part, I had rather ſell myſelf to ſomebody elſe.

Touchit. And why ſo, Mr. Mayor?

Mayor. I don't know—they do a mortal deal of harm in the country: Why, wherever any of them ſettles, it raiſes the price of proviſions for thirty miles round. People rail at ſeaſons and crops; in my opinion, it is all along with them there folks, that things are ſo ſcarce.

Touchit.

Touchit. Why, you talk like a fool! Suppofe they have mounted the beef and mutton a trifle; a'n't we obliged to them too for raifing the value of boroughs? You fhould always fet one againft t'other.

Mayor. That, indeed, is nothing but fair. But how comes it about? and where do thefe here people get all their wealth?

Touchit. The way is plain enough; from our fettlements and poffeffions abroad.

Mayor. Oh, may be fo. I've been often minded to afk you what fort of things them there fettlements are; becaufe why, as you know, I have been never beyond fea.

Touchit. Oh, Mr. Mayor, I will explain that in a moment: Why, here are a body of merchants that beg to be admitted as friends, and take poffeffion of a fmall fpot in a country, and carry on a beneficial commerce with the inoffenfive and innocent people, to which they kindly give their confent.

Mayor. Don't you think now that is very civil of them?

Touchit. Doubtlefs. Upon which, Mr. Mayor, we cunningly encroach, and fortify by little and by little, till at length, we growing too ftrong for the natives, we turn them out of their lands, and take poffeffion of their money and jewels.

Mayor.

Mayor. And don't you think, Mafter Touchit, that is a little uncivil in us?

Touchit. Oh, nothing at all: Thefe people are but a little better than Tartars or Turks.

Mayor. No, no, Mafter Touchit; juft the reverfe; it is *they* have caught the Tartars in us.

Touchit. Ha, ha, ha! well faid, Mr. Mayor. But, hufh! here comes his honour. Fall back!

Enter Sir Matthew Mite.

Mite. Oh, Nathan! are you there? You have fplit the ftock, as I bid you?

Nathan. I vas punctually obey your directions.

Mite. And I fhall be in no danger of lofing my lift?

Nathan. Dat is fafe, your honour; we have noting to fear.

Mite. Mofes Mendoza! You will take care to qualify Peter Pratewell and Counfellor Quibble? I fhall want fome fpeakers at the next General Court.

Mofes. Pleafe your honour, I fhall be careful of dat.

Mite. How is the ftock?

Mofes. It vas got up the end of the veek.

Mite. Then fell out till you fink it two and a half. Has my advice been followed for burning the tea?

Mofes.

Moses. As to dat matter, I vas not enquire dat; I believe not.

Mite. So that commodity will soon be a drug. The English are too proud to profit by the practice of others: What would become of the spice trade, if the Dutch brought their whole growth to market?

Moses. Dat is very true. Your honour has no farder commands?

Mite. None at present, master Mendoza.

[*Exit Mendoza.*

Nathan. For de next settlement, would your honour be de bull or de bear?

Mite. I shall send you my orders to Jonathan's. Oh, Nathan! did you tell that man in Berkshire, I would buy his estate?

Nathan. Yes; but he say he has no mind, no occasion to sell it; dat de estate belong to great many faders before him.

Mite. Why, the man must be mad; did you tell him I had taken a fancy to the spot, when I was but a boy?

Nathan. I vas tell him as much.

Mite. And that all the time I was in India, my mind was bent upon the purchase?

Nathan. I vas say so.

Mite. And now I'm come home, am determined to buy it?

G

Nathan.

Nathan. I make ufe of de very vords.

Mite. Well then! what would the booby be at?

Nathan. I don't know.

Mite. Give the fellow four times the value, and bid him turn out in a month.—[*To Touchit.*] May I prefume, Sir, to afk who you are, and what your bufinefs may be?

Touchit. My name, Sir, is Touchit, and thefe gentlemen fome friends and neighbours of mine. We are ordered by the Chriftian Club, of the borough of Bribe'em, to wait upon your honour, with a tender of the nomination of our two members at the enfuing election.

Mite. Sir, I accept their offer with pleafure; and am happy to find, notwithftanding all that has been faid, that the union ftill fubfifts between Bengal and the ancient corporation of Bribe'em.

Touchit. And if they ever are fevered, I can affure your honour the Chriftian Club will not be to blame. Your honour underftands me, I hope?

Mite. Perfectly. Nor fhall it, I promife you, be my fault, good Mr. Touchit. But, (you will forgive my curiofity, Sir!) the name your club has adopted, has at firft a whimfical found; but you had your reafons, no doubt.

Touchit. The very belt in the world, pleafe

your

your honour: From our ſtrict union and bro-
therly kindneſs, we hang together; like the
primitive Chriſtians too, we have all things in
common.

Mite. In common? I don't apprehend you.

Touchit. Why, pleaſe your honour, when the
bargain is ſtruck, and the depoſit is made, as a
proof that we love our neighbours as well as
ourſelves, we ſubmit to an equal partition; no
man has a larger ſhare than another.

Mite. A moſt Chriſtian-like diſpenſation!

Touchit. Yes; in our borough all is unanimity
now: Formerly, we had nothing but diſcontents
and heart-burnings amongſt us; each man jealous and afraid that his neighbour got more and
did better than him.

Mite. Indeed?

Touchit. Ay, and with reaſon ſometimes.
Why, I remember, at the election ſome time ago,
when I took up my freedom, I could get but
thirty guineas for a new pair of jack-boots;
whilſt Tom Ramſkin over the way had a fifty-
pound note for a pair of waſh-leather breeches.

Mite. Very partial indeed!

Touchit. So, upon the whole, we thought it
beſt to unite.

Mite. Oh, much the beſt. Well, Sir, you
may aſſure your principals that I ſhall take care

properly

properly to acknowledge the fervice they do me.

Touchit. No doubt, no doubt. But—will your honour ftep a little this way ?—Though no queftion can be made of your honour's keeping your word, yet it has always been the rule with our club to receive the proper acknowledgment before the fervice is done.

Mite. Ay, but, Mr. Touchit, fuppofe the fervice fhould never be done?

Touchit. What then muft become of our confciences ? We are Chriftians, your honour.

Mite. True ; but, Mr. Touchit, you remember the proverb ?

Touchit. What proverb, your honour ?

Mite. There are two bad pay-mafters ; thofe who pay before, and thofe who never pay.

Touchit. True, your honour ; but our club has always found, that thofe who don't pay before are fure never to pay.

Mite. How ! impoffible ! the man who breaks his word with fuch faithful and honeft adherents, deferves richly a halter. Gentlemen, in my opinion, he deferves to be hanged.

Touchit. Hufh ! have a care what you fay.

Mite. What is the matter ?

Touchit. You fee the fat man that is behind ; he will be the returning officer at the election,

Mite.

Mite. What then?

Touchit. On a gibbet at the end of our town there hangs a smuggler, for robbing the custom-house.

Mite. Well?

Touchit. The mayor's own brother, your honour: Now, perhaps, he may be jealous that you meant to throw some reflection on him or his family.

Mite. Not unlikely.—I say, gentlemen, whoever violates his promise to such faithful friends as you are, in my poor opinion, deserves to be damned!

Touchit. That's right! stick to that! for tho' the Christian Club may have some fears of the gallows, they don't value damnation of a farthing.

Mite. Why should they, as it may be so long before any thing of that kind may happen, you know?

Touchit. Good! good again! Your honour takes us rightly, I see: I make no doubt, it won't be long before we come to a good understanding.

Mite. The sooner the better, good master Touchit; and, therefore, in one word, pray what are your terms?

Touchit. Do you mean for one, or would your honour bargain for both?

Mite.

Mite. Both, both.

Touchit. Why, we could not have afforded you one under three thousand at least; but as your honour, as I may say, has a mind to deal in the grofs, we shall charge you but five for both.

Mite. Oh fy! above the market, good Mr. Touchit!

Touchit. Dog-cheap; neck-beef; a penny-loaf for a halfpenny! Why, we had partly agreed to bring in Sir Chriftopher Quinze and major Match'em for the very fame money; but the major has been a little unlucky at Almack's, and at prefent can't depofit the needful; but he fays, however, if he fhould be fuccefsful at the next Newmarket meeting, he will faithfully abide by the bargain: But the turf, your honour knows, is but an uncertain eftate, and fo we can't depend upon him.

Mite. True. Well, Sir, as I may foon have occafion for all the friends I can make, I fhall haggle no longer; I accept your propofals: In the next room we will fettle the terms.

Touchit. Your honour will always find the Chriftians fteady and firm.—But, won't your honour introduce us to his Worfhip whilft we are here?

Mite. To his Worfhip? to whom?

Touchit. To the gentleman in black.

Mite.

Mite. Worfhip? you are mad, Mr. Touchit! That is a flave I brought from the Indies.

Touchit. Good lack! may be fo! I did not know but the gentleman might belong to the tribe, who, we are told by the papers, conferred thofe fplendid titles upon your honour in India.

Mite. Well, Mafter Touchit, what then?

Touchit. I thought it not unlikely, but, in return to that compliment, your honour might chufe to make one of the family member for the corporation of Bribe'em.

Mite. Why, you would not fubmit to accept of a Negro?

Touchit. Our prefent members, for aught we know, may be of the fame complexion, your honour; for we have never fet eyes on them yet.

Mite. That's ftrange! But, after all, you could not think of electing a black?

Touchit. That makes no difference to us: The Chriftian Club has ever been perfuaded, that a good candidate, like a good horfe, can't be of a bad colour.   [*Exit with friends.*

Enter Thomas Oldham and others.

Mite [*to Oldham*]. What is your bufinefs, and name?

Thomas. Oldham.

Mite.

Mite. The brother of Sir John ? I have heard of you : You are, if I miftake not; a merchant ?

Thomas. I have that honour, Sir Matthew.

Mite. Um ! honour !—Well, Sir; and what are your commands ?

Thomas. I wait on you in the name of my brother, with——

Mite. An anfwer to the meffage I fent him. When do we meet to finifh the matter ? It muft be tomorrow, or Sunday; for I fhall be bufy next week.

Thomas. Tomorrow ?

Mite. Ay; it is not for a man like me to dangle and court; Mr. Oldham.

Thomas. Why, to be plain, Sir Matthew, it would, I am afraid; be but lofing your time.

Mite. Sir ?

Thomas. As there is not one in the family, that feems the leaft inclined to favour your wifh.

Mite. No? ha, ha, ha ! that's pleafant enough ! ha, ha, ha ! And why not ?

Thomas. They are, Sir Matthew, no ftrangers to your great power and wealth; but corrupt as you may conceive this country to be, there are fuperior fpirits living, who would difdain an Alliance with grandeur obtained at the expence of honour and virtue.

Mite.

Mite. And what relation has this fentimental declaration to me ?

Thomas. My intention, Sir Matthew, was not to offend ; I was defired to wait on you with a civil denial.

Mite. And you have faithfully difcharged your commiffion.

Thomas. Why, I'm a man of plain manners, Sir Matthew ; a fupercilious air, or a fneer, won't prevent me from fpeaking my thoughts.

Mite. Perfectly right, and prodigioufly prudent !—Well, Sir ; I hope it won't be thought too prefuming, if I defire to hear my fentence proceed from the mouth of the father and daughter,

Thomas. By all means ; I will wait on you thither.

Mite. That is not fo convenient, at prefent. I have brought from Italy, antiques, fome curious remains, which are to be depofited in the archives of this country : The Antiquarian Society have, in confequence, chofen me one of their body, and this is the hour of reception.

Thomas. We fhall fee you in the courfe of the day ?

Mite. At the clofe of the ceremony. Perhaps, I fhall have fomething to urge, that may procure me fome favour from your very refpectable

H   family,—

family.—Piccard, attend Mr. A—a—a to the door.

Thomas. I guefs your defign.   [*Exit.*
Mite. Who waits there?

Enter Servant.

Step to my attorney directly; bid him attend me within an hour at Oldham's, armed with all the powers I gave him.   [*Exit Servant.*
I will fee if I can't bend to my will this fturdy race of infolent beggars !—After all, riches to a man who knows how to employ them, are as ufeful in England as in any part of the Eaft : There they gain us thofe ends in fpite and defiance of law, which, with a proper agent, may here be obtained under the pretence and colour of law.

        [*Exit.*

ACT III.

The Antiquarian Society.

Secretary.

SIR Matthew Mite, preceded by his prefents, will attend this honourable Society this morning.

1 *Ant.* Is he apprifed that an inauguration-fpeech is required, in which he is to exprefs his love of vertù, and produce proofs of his antique erudition?

Sec. He has been apprifed, and is rightly prepared.

2 *Ant.* Are the minutes of our laft meeting fairly recorded and entered?

Sec. They are.

1 *Ant.* And the valuable antiques which have happily efcaped the depredations of time ranged and regiftered rightly?

Sec. All in order.

2 *Ant.* As there are new acquifitions to the Society's ftock, I think it is right that the members fhould be inftructed in their feveral natures and names.

1 *Ant.* By all means. Read the lift!

Sec. " *Imprimis,* In a large glafs-cafe, and in " fine prefervation, the toe of the flipper of

" Cardinal Pandulpho, with which he kick'd the
" breech of King John at Swinſtead-Abbey, when
" he gave him abſolution and penance."

2 *Ant.* A moſt noble remains!

1 *Ant.* An excellent antidote againſt the pro-
greſs of Popery, as it proves the Pontiff's inſo-
lent abuſe of his power!—Proceed.

Sec. " A pair of nut-crackers preſented by
" Harry the Eighth to Anna Bullen the eve of
" their nuptials; the wood ſuppoſed to be
" walnut."

1 *Ant.* Which proves that before the Reforma-
tion walnut-trees were planted in England.

Sec. " The cape of Queen Elizabeth's riding-
" hood, which ſhe wore on a ſolemn feſtival,
" when carried behind Burleigh to Paul's; the
" cloth undoubtedly Kidderminſter."

2 *Ant.* A moſt inſtructive leſſon to us, as it
proves that patriotic princeſs wore nothing but
the manufactures of England!

Sec. " A cork-ſcrew preſented by Sir John
" Falſtaff to Harry the Fifth, with a tobacco-
" ſtopper of Sir Walter Raleigh's, made of the
" ſtern of the ſhip in which he firſt compaſſed
" the globe; given to the Society by a clergy-
" man from the North-Riding of Yorkſhire."

1 *Ant.* A rare inſtance of generoſity, as they
muſt have both been of ſingular uſe to the reverend donor himſelf!

Sec.

Sec. " A curious collection, in regular and
" undoubted fucceſſion, of all the tickets of
" Iſlington-Turnpike, from its firſt inſtitution
" to the twentieth of May."

2 *Ant.* Preſerve them with care, as they may
hereafter ſerve to illuſtrate that part of the
Engliſh Hiſtory.

Sec. " A wooden medal of Shakeſpeare, made
" from the mulberry-tree he planted himſelf; with
" a Queen Anne's farthing; from the Manager of
" Drury-Lane Playhouſe."

1 *Ant.* Has he received the Society's thanks ?
Sec. They are ſent.

Enter Beadle.

Beadle. Sir Matthew Mite attends at the door.
1 *Ant.* Let him be admitted directly.

*Enter Sir Matthew Mite, preceded by four Blacks;
firſt Black bearing a large book; ſecond, a green
chamber-pot; third, ſome lava from the mountain
Veſuvius; fourth, a box. Sir Matthew takes his
ſeat; Secretary receives the firſt preſent, and reads
the label.*

Sec. " Purchaſed of the Abbé Montini at
" Naples for five hundred pounds, an illegible
" manuſcript in Latin, containing the twelve
" books of Livy, ſuppoſed to be loſt."

Mite.

Mite. This invaluable treafure was very near falling into the hands of the Pope, who defigned to depofit it in the Vatican Library, and I re-fcued it from idolatrous hands:

1 *Ant.* A pious, learned, and laudable pur-chafe!

Sec. [*receives the fecond prefent, and reads the label.*] " A farcophagus, or Roman urn, dug " from the temple of Concord."

Mite. Suppofed to have held the duft of Marc-Antony's coachman.

Sec. [*receives the third prefent, and reads.*] " A " large piece of the lava, thrown from the Vefuvian " volcano at the laft great eruption."

Mite. By a chymical analyfis, it will be eafy to difcover the conftituent parts of this mafs; which, by properly preparing it, will make it no difficult tafk to propagate burning mountains in England, if encouraged by premiums.

2 *Ant.* Which it will, no doubt!

Mite. Gentlemen! Not contented with col-lecting, for the ufe of my country, thefe inefti-mable relics, with a large catalogue of petri-factions, bones, beetles, and butterflies, con-tained in that box, [*pointing to the prefent borne by the fourth Black.*] I have likewife laboured for the advancement of national knowledge: For which end, permit me to clear up fome doubts relative to a material and interefting point in the

English

English history. Let others toil to illumine the dark annals of Greece, or of Rome; my searches are sacred only to the service of Britain !

The point I mean to clear up, is an error crept into the life of that illustrious magistrate, the great Whittington, and his no-less-eminent Cat: And in this disquisition four material points are in question.

1st. Did Whittington ever exist?

2d. Was Whittington Lord-Mayor of London?

3d. Was he really possessed of a Cat?

4th. Was that Cat the source of his wealth?

That Whittington lived, no doubt can be made; that he was Lord-Mayor of London, is equally true; but as to his Cat, that, gentlemen, is the gordian knot to untie. And here, gentlemen, be it permitted me to define what a Cat is. A Cat is a domestic, whiskered, four-footed animal, whose employment is catching of mice; but let Puss have been ever so subtle, let Puss have been ever so successful, to what could Puss's captures amount? no tanner can curry the skin of a mouse, no family make a meal of the meat; consequently, no Cat could give Whittington his wealth. From whence then does this error proceed? be that my care to point out !

The commerce this worthy merchant carried
on,

on, was chiefly confined to our coasts; for
this purpose, he constructed a vessel, which, from
its agility and lightness, he aptly christened a
Cat.   Nay, to this our day, gentlemen, all our
coals from Newcastle are imported in nothing
but Cats.   From thence it appears, that it was
not the whiskered, four-footed, mouse-killing Cat,
that was the source of the magistrate's wealth,
but the coasting, sailing, coal-carrying Cat; that,
gentlemen, was Whittington's Cat.

  1 *Ant.* What a fund of learning!

  2 *Ant.* Amazing acuteness of erudition!

  1 *Ant.* Let this discovery be made public
directly.

  2 *Ant.* And the author mentioned with honour.

  1 *Ant.* I make no doubt but the city of London will desire him to sit for his picture, or send
him his freedom in a fifty-pound box.

  2 *Ant.* The honour done their first magistrate
richly deserves it.

  1 *Ant.* Break we up this assembly, with a loud
declaration, that Sir Matthew Mite is equally
skilled in arts as well as in arms.

  2 *Ant. Tam Mercurio quam Marti.* [*Exe. Ant.*

  Mite. Having thus discharged my debt to the
public, I must attend to my private affairs. Will
Rapine, my attorney, attend as I bid him?

                                                    Serv.

Serv. He will be punctual, your honour.

Mite. Then drive to Hanover-Square.

Putty [*without*]. I will come in!

Enter Servant.

Serv. There's a little shabby fellow without, that insists on seeing your honour.

Mite. Why, who and what can he be?

Serv. He calls himself Putty, and says he went to school with your honour.

Serv. [*within.*] His honour don't know you!

Putty. I will come in! Not know me, you oaf? what should ail him? Why, I tell you we were bred up together from boys. Stand by, or I'll——

Enter Putty.

Hey! yes, it is—no, it a'n't—yes, it is Matthew Mite.—Lord love your queer face! what a figure you cut! how you are altered! well, had I met with you by chance, I don't think I should ever have known you. I have had a deuced deal of work to get at you.

Mite. This is a lucky encounter!

Putty. There is a little fat fellow, that opens the door at your house, was as pert as a prentice just out of his time: He would not give me the least inkling about you; and I should have re-

I   turned

turned to Shoreditch as wife as I came, if fome folks who are gazing at the fine gilt coach in the ftreet, hadn't told me 'twas yours. Well, Mafter Mite, things are mainly changed fince we were boys at the Blue-Coat: Who could have thought that you would have got fo up in the world? for you know you were reckoned a dull one at fchool.

Serv. Friend, do you know who you talk to?

Putty. Yes, friend, much better than you do. I am told he is become a Knight, and a Nabob; and what of all that? For your Nabobs, they are but a kind of outlandifh creatures, that won't pafs current with us; and as to knights, we have a few of them in the city, whom I dare fpeak to without doffing my hat. So, Mr. Scrape-trencher, let's have no more of your jaw!—I fay, Mat, doefn't remember one Eafter-Tuefday, how you tipt the barrow-woman into Fleet-Ditch, as we were going about with the hymns?

Mite. An anecdote that does me infinite honour!

Putty. How all the folks laughed to fee how bolt upright fhe ftood on her head in the mud! ha! ha! ha! And one fifth of November, I fhall never forget! how you frightened a preaching methodift taylor, by throwing a cracker into the pulpit.

Mite.

Mite. Another pretty exploit!

Putty. At every bounce, how poor Stitch ca-
pered and jumped! Ah! many's the merry freak
we have had! for this I muſt ſay, though Mat
was but bad at his book, for miſchiefful matters there waſn't a more ingenous, cuterer lad in
the ſchool.

Mite. Yes; I have got a fine reputation, I ſee!

Putty. Well, but Mat! what, be'ſt dumb?
why doeſn't ſpeak to a ſchool-fellow?

Mite. That at preſent is more than I'll own.——
I fancy, Mr. A--a--a, you have made ſome
miſtake.

Putty. Some miſtake?

Mite. I don't recollect that I ever had the honour to know you.

Putty. What, don't you remember Phil Putty?

Mite. No.

Putty. That was prentice to Maſter Gibſon,
the glazier in Shoreditch?

Mite. No.

Putty. That at the Blue-Coat-Hoſpital has
often ſaved your bacon by owning your pranks?

Mite. No.

Putty. No! What, then, mayhap you ben't
Mat Mite, ſon of old John and Margery Mite,
at the Sow and Sauſage in St. Mary Axe, that
took the tarts from the man in Pye-corner, and

was fent beyond fea, for fear worfe fhould come on it?

Mite. You fee, Mr. Putty, the glazier, if that is your name and profeffion, you are entirely out in this matter; fo you need not repeat your vifits to me.   [*Exit.*

Putty. Now here's a pretty purfe-proud fon of a——who, forfooth, becaufe he is grown great by robbing the heathens, won't own an old friend and acquaintance, and one too of the livery befide! Dammee, the great Turk himfelf need not be afhamed to fhake hands with a citizen! " Mr. Putty the glazier!" well, what a pox am I the better for you ? I'll be fworn our company has made more money by a fingle election at Brentford, than by all his exploits put together.   [*Exit.*

Sir John Oldham's houfe.

Enter Mr. Thomas Oldham, followed by a Servant.

Thomas. Sir Matthew Mite is not come ?

Serv. No, Sir.

Thomas. Is Tom here?

Serv. Mr. Oldham is, I believe, with Mifs in the parlour.

Thomas. Let him know I would fee him. [*Exit Serv.*] Poor boy! Nay, I fincerely grieve for them both! this difappointment, like an

untimely

untimely froſt, will hang heavy on their tender years : To conquer the firſt and fineſt feelings of nature is an arduous taſk !

Enter Young Oldham.

So, Tom ! ſtill attached to this ſpot, I perceive ?

Y. Old. Sir, I arrived but the inſtant before you.

Thomas. Nay, child, I don't blame you. You are no ſtranger to the almoſt-invincible bars that oppoſe your views on my niece; it would be therefore prudent, inſtead of indulging, to wean yourſelf by degrees.

Y. Old. Are there no hopes, then, Sir, of ſubduing my aunt ?

Thomas. I ſee none : Nay, perhaps, as matters now ſtand, a compliance may be out of her power.

Y. Old. How is that poſſible, Sir ? out of her power ?

Thomas. I won't anticipate : Misfortunes come too ſoon of themſelves ; a ſhort time will explain what I mean.

Y. Old. You alarm me ! Would you condeſcend to inſtruct me, I hope, Sir, I ſhall have diſcretion enough——

Thomas. It would anſwer no end. I would have you both prepare for the worſt : See your
couſin

couſin again; and remember, this, perhaps, may be the laſt time of your meeting.

Y. Old. The laſt of our——

Thomas. But Sophy is here. I muſt go in to Sir John. [*Oldham bows low to Sophy and retires.*

Enter Sophy.

Sophy. Sir! What can be the meaning of this? My uncle Oldham avoids me! you ſeem ſhocked! no additional misfortune, I hope?

Y. Old. My father has threatened me, in obſcure terms, I confeſs, with the worſt that can happen.

Sophy. How!

Y. Old. The total, nay, perhaps, immediate loſs of my Sophy.

Sophy. From what cauſe?

Y. Old. That in tenderneſs he choſe to conceal.

Sophy. But why make it a myſtery? have you no gueſs?

Y. Old. Not the moſt diſtant conception. My lady's diſlike would hardly prompt her to ſuch violent meaſures. I can't comprehend how this can poſſibly be; but yet my father has too firm, too manly a mind, to encourage or harbour vain fears.

Sophy. Here they come. I ſuppoſe the riddle will ſoon be explained.

Enter

Enter Sir John, Lady, and Thomas Oldham.

L. Old. But what motive could he have for demanding this whimfical interview? he could not doubt your credentials, or think his prefence could be grateful to us.

Thomas. I have delivered my meffage.

L. Old. Perhaps he depends on his rhetorical powers: I hear he has a good opinion of them. Stay, Sophy! Sir Matthew Mite, diftrufting the meffage we begged your uncle to carry, defires to have it confirmed by ourfelves: I fancy, child, you will do yourfelf no violence in rejecting this lover. He is an amiable fwain, I confefs!

Sophy. I fhall be always happy in obeying your ladyfhip's orders.

L. Old. Are you fure of that, Sophy? a time may foon come for the trial.

Sir John. Well, in the main, I am glad of this meeting; it will not only put a final end to this bufinefs, but give us an opportunity of difcuffing other matters, my dear.

L. Old. Is that your opinion, Sir John? I fancy he will not be very fond of prolonging his vifit.

Enter Servant.

Serv. Sir Matthew Mite!

L. Old.

L. Old. Shew him in!—Now, Sir John, be on your guard; fupport this fcene with a dignity that becomes one of your birth and——

Sir John. Never fear my dignity, love. I warrant you I'll give him as good as he brings.

Enter Sir Matthew Mite.

Mite. I find the whole tribe is convened.—I hope I am not an intruder; but I confefs the extraordinary anfwer I received from the mouth of this worthy citizen, to a meffage conveyed by my fecretary, induced me to queftion its authenticity, unlefs confirmed by yourfelves.

L. Old. And why fhould you think our reply fo very extraordinary?

Mite. You muft give me leave to fmile at that queftion.

L. Old. A very decifive anfwer, I own!

Mite. You are, Lady Oldham, a woman of the world, and fuppofed not to be wanting in fenfe.

L. Old. Which this conduct of mine inclines you to doubt?

Mite. Why, to be plain, my condition and your own fituation confidered, prudence might have dictated a different reply.

L. Old. And yet, Sir Matthew, upon the matureft deliberation, all the parties, you fee, perfift in giving no other.

Mite.

Mite. Is it so? You will permit me, Lady Oldham, to defire one of thofe reafons which influenced this auguft affembly upon the occafion?

L. Old. They will, I dare fay, appear but trifling to you.

Mite. Let us have them, however.

L. Old. Firft, we think it right to have a little regard to *her* happinefs, as fhe is indebted for her exiftence to us.

Mite. Which you think fhe rifques in a union with me? [*Lady Oldham bows.*] And why fo? I have the means to procure her, madam, thofe enjoyments with which your fex is chiefly delighted.

L. Old. You will, Sir Matthew, pardon my weaknefs; but I would much rather fee my child with a competence, nay, even reduced to an indigent ftate, than voluptuoufly rioting in pleafures that derive their fource from the ruin of others.

Mite. Ruin! what, you, I find, adopt the popular prejudice, and conclude that every man that is rich is a villain?

L. Old. I only echo the voice of the public. Befides, I would wifh my daughter a more folid eftablifhment: The poffeffions arifing from plunder very rarely are permanent; we every day fee what has been treacheroufly and rapacioufly gained, as profufely and full as rapidly fquandered.

K   *Mite.*

Mite. I am forry, madam, to fee one of your fafhion, concur in the common cry of the times; but fuch is the gratitude of this country to thofe who have given it dominion and wealth.

Thomas. I could wifh even that fact was well founded, Sir Matthew. Your riches (which perhaps too are only ideal) by introducing a general fpirit of diffipation, have extinguifhed labour and induftry, the flow, but fure fource of national wealth.

Mite. To thefe refinements I have no time to reply. By one of your ladyfhip's hints I fhall profit at leaft: I fhall be a little more careful of the plunder I have made. Sir John Oldham, you recollect a fmall fum borrowed by you?

Sir John. I do.

Mite. The obligations for which are in my poffeffion at prefent.

Sir John. I underftand as much by your letter.

Mite. As I find there is an end of our treaty, it would be right, I think, to difcharge them directly.

Sir John. I can't fay that is quite fo convenient; befides, I underftood the party was to wait till the time that Jack comes of age.

Mite. I am told the law does not underftand what is not clearly expreffed. Befides, the probable event of your death, or the young gentleman's
shynefs

shyness to fulfil the agreement, are enough to put a man on his guard.

Thomas. Now comes on the storm.

Mite. And, that my prudence might not suffer in that lady's opinion, I have taken some precautions which my attorney will more clearly unfold.—Mr. Rapine !

Enter Rapine.

You will explain this affair to Sir John : I am a military man, and quite a stranger to your legal manœuvres.

Rap. By command of my client, Sir Matthew, I have issued here a couple of writs.

L. Old. Sir John !

Sir John. What ?

Rap. By one of which, plaintiff possesses the person, by t'other goods and chattels, of Sir John the defendant.

Mite. A definition very clear and concise !

L. Old. Goods, Sir ? what, must I be turned out of my house ?

Rap. No, madam ; you may stay here till we sell, which perhaps mayn't happen these two days. We must, indeed, leave a few of our people, just to take care that there is nothing embezzled.

L. Old. A short respite, indeed ! For a little

time,

time, I dare fay, my brother Oldham will afford us protection. Come, Sir John, nor let us indulge that monfter's malice with a longer fight of our mifery.

Rap. You, madam, are a wife, and may go where you pleafe; but as to Sir John——

L. Old. Well!

Rap. He muft not ftir: We are anfwerable for the pofieffion of him.

L. Old. Of him? a prifoner? then indeed is our ruin complete!

Sophy. Oh, uncle!—You have been pleafed, Sir, to exprefs an affection for me: Is it poffible, Sir, you can be fo cruel, fo unkind to my parents——

Mite. They are unkind to themfelves.

Sophy. Let me plead for mercy! fufpend but a little!—My uncle, you, Sir, are wealthy too!—Indeed we are honeft! you will not run the leaft rifque.

Mite. There is a condition, Mifs, in which you have a right to command.

Sophy. Sir!.

Mite. It is in your power, and that of your parents, to eftablifh one common intereft amongft us.

L. Old. Never! after rejecting, with the contempt they deferved, the firft arrogant offers you made, do you fuppofe this frefh infult will gain us?

Mite.

Mite. I am anfwered.—I prefume, Mr. Rapine, there is no longer occafion for me?

Sophy. Stop, Sir! Mr. Oldham teaches me what I fhould do. Can I fee their diftrefs? Heaven knows with what eagernefs I would facrifice my own peace, my own happinefs, to procure them relief!   [*Kneels to Sir Matthew.*

Thomas. Rife, niece! nor hope to foften that breaft, already made too callous by crimes! I have long feen, Sir, what your malice intended, and prepared myfelf to baffle its purpofe. I am inftructed, Sir, in the amount of this man's demands on my brother: You will there find a fum more than fufficient to pay it.—And now, my dear fifter, I hope you will pleafe to allow a citizen may be ufeful fometimes.

Mite. Mr. Rapine, is this manœuvre according to law?

Rap. The law, Sir Matthew, always fleeps when fatisfaction is made.

Mite. Does it? Our practice is different in the Mayor's Court at Calcutta.—I fhall now make my bow; and leave this family, whom I wifhed to make happy in fpite of themfelves, foon to regret the fatal lofs fuftained by their obftinate folly.

Thomas. Nor can it be long, before the wifdom of their choice will appear; as by partaking of

the

the fpoil, they might have been involved in that
vengeance, which foon or late can't fail to fall on
the head of the author: And, Sir, notwithftanding
your feeming fecurity, perhaps the hour of re-
tribution is near !

Mite. You muft, Mafter Oldham, give me leave
to laugh at your prophetic effufion. This is not
Sparta, nor are thefe the chafte times of the Roman
republic : Now-a-days, riches poffefs at leaft
one magical power, that, being rightly difpenfed,
they clofely conceal the fource from whence they
proceeded : That wifdom, I hope never to want.—
I am the obfequious fervant of this refpectable
family ! Adieu !—Come along, Rapine !

[*Exit with Rapine.*

L. Old. Brother, what words can I ufe, or how
can we thank you as we ought ? Sir John ! Sophy !

Thomas. I am doubly paid, Lady Oldham, in .
fupplying the wants of my friends, and defeating
the defigns of a villain. As to the mere money,
we citizens indeed are odd kind of folks, and
always expect good fecurity for what we advance.

L. Old. Sir John's perfon, his fortune, every——

Thomas. Nay, nay, nay, upon this occafion we
will not be troubled with land : If you, fifter,
will place as a pledge my fair coufin in the hands
of my fon——

L. Old. I freely refign her difpofal to you.

Sir

Sir John. And I.

Thomas. Then be happy, my children! And as to my young coufins within, I hope we fhall be able to fettle them without Sir Matthew's affiftance: For, however praifeworthy the fpirit of adventure may be, whoever keeps his poft, and does his duty at home, will be found to render his country beft fervice at laft! [*Exeunt.*

F I N I S.

Juſt Publiſhed,

The C O M·E D I.E S of

The Cozeners;

(Containing Two Original Scenes, not
inſerted in the ſpurious Impreſſions)

The Maid of Bath;

A N D

The Devil Upon Two Sticks.

All written by the ſame Author,

And publiſhed by the ſame Editor.

And in a few Days will be Publiſhed,

The Tailors;

A TRAGEDY for WARM WEATHER.

As it is Performed at the Theatre-Royal, Haymarket.

www.ingramcontent.com/pod-product-compliance
Lightning Source LLC
Chambersburg PA
CBHW030003030726
47499CB00008B/2871